MONSTRUM HOUSE

Author dedication:
To Jugs, because Trapper and Scout can't read

Monstrum House: Creeped Out
published in 2010 by
Hardie Grant Egmont
85 High Street
Prahran, Victoria 3181, Australia
www.hardiegrantegmont.com.au

A CiP record for this title is available from the National Library of Australia

Text copyright © 2010 Zana Fraillon
Illustration and design copyright © 2010 Hardie Grant Egmont

Design and illustration by Simon Swingler
Typeset by Ektavo

Printed in Australia by McPherson's Printing Group

1 3 5 7 9 10 8 6 4 2

Creeped Out

By Zana Fraillon

Illustrations by Simon Swingler

hardie grant EGMONT

Jasper McPhee looked at the door. It looked just like a normal classroom door. But he knew that on the other side of it was a room that was anything *but* normal.

Jasper pushed open the door and stepped inside the pitch-black room, flinching slightly as the door swung shut behind him. He knew what was waiting for him in the dark. It took all his willpower not to run straight out of the room again.

His eyes had adjusted to the gloom now.

He could just make out the Quiddlesquawk slinking towards him. It crept low along the floor. It was close enough for him to see the glowing red slits of its eyes in the darkness. Jasper took a deep breath and shook the fear from his body.

The trick was to stay still and not panic.

Jasper could feel a buzz of excitement beginning to shoot through his body. The monster moved even closer. But Jasper wasn't frightened anymore. He was ready.

Jasper could feel the weight of the rope in his Hunt belt. He went into Hunt position. Legs slightly bent, arms spread, every muscle quivering in readiness. He clenched his teeth and then leapt, springing up and over the monster's head.

He landed squarely on the monster's back, his head facing towards its tail. He wrapped

Quiddlesquawk

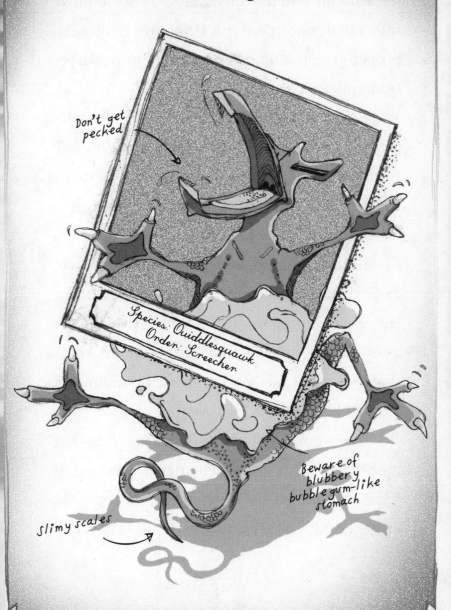

his arms around its slimy scales, trying to move into a better position. But before he could get a proper grip, the monster rolled, pinning Jasper underneath it.

Jasper had learnt enough about Quiddlesquawks in Species Studies to expect it to roll. But learning about a monster and actually catching one were two very different things.

As the monster got ready to suffocate him under its blubbery bubblegum-like stomach, Jasper snaked his arm towards its eye socket. He didn't want to think about its eyes. Monster eyes always freaked him out. And he knew that fear was exactly what the Quiddlesquawk wanted him to feel.

Jasper poked his finger sharply into the monster's eye. It squawked angrily, twisting its head around and snapping its razor-sharp beak at his hand. The shift in the monster's weight was just enough for Jasper to slip out from under it.

Within three seconds, Jasper had grabbed the rope from his Hunt belt and bound it around the monster's beak. He strapped its beak to its body, then flipped the monster onto its back.

He couldn't help feeling just a little bit cool.

A glowing exit sign appeared in the dark.

'Your score is eighty-four per cent,' Stenka's severe voice announced over the intercom. 'Proceed to the exit.'

Stenka was Jasper's homeroom teacher. Of all the teachers at Monstrum House, Jasper reckoned Stenka was probably the scariest. It was not a good idea to get on her wrong side.

Eighty-four per cent, thought Jasper, wiping the slime from his hands. *Not great – but not too bad*.

He already knew where he had gone wrong.

He hadn't thought about the slipperiness of the monster when he'd leapt.

'Proceed to the exit,' Stenka ordered again.

Jasper bent down to inspect the monster. He almost felt sorry for the thing. After all, he knew the Quiddlesquawk had been trained by the teachers. And really, what kind of life was it, battling annoying kids all day long?

Jasper forced himself to look it in the eyes. One eye looked sore and bloodshot.

'Sorry, fella,' he whispered. He loosened the rope he'd tied around its beak.

The monster blinked and for a second its empty eyes took on a deeper glint of understanding. Then it opened its mouth and spat a long line of slime over Jasper's face. Jasper gagged.

'Next time you should do as you're told,' said Stenka smugly over the intercom.

Jasper glared at the monster. There was a foul fishy taste in his mouth and his eyes stung like they were full of soap.

'Thanks a lot,' he mumbled darkly, and left the room.

Jasper had been at the Monstrum House School for Troubled Children for about six months.

Monstrum House was not like any school Jasper had ever been to, and he'd been to a lot of schools. At this school, instead of learning how to read, write and do maths, the students were only taught one thing: how to hunt monsters.

The school building was an old stone mansion with towering turrets and plate-glass windows, surrounded by a spooky dark forest. None of the kids knew exactly where the school was, or even which country it was in. They had all been flown to the school in some kind of hypnotised sleep, and had no idea how far from their homes they were. But wherever they were, it was cold. Not just cold – freezing. It snowed all the time. And the area was crawling with monsters. Jasper wondered if the monsters somehow created the chilly weather – whenever they were about the temperature seemed to drop.

Jasper hadn't yet worked out if he was more scared of the monsters or the teachers. He was pretty sure the teachers at Monstrum House could read his thoughts. They had a spooky way of knowing what you were thinking. And of course, if you did anything wrong, they could tell – and you'd be punished.

Jasper had been expelled from every school he'd ever been to. He was used to school punishments. But at Monstrum House, being punished didn't mean picking up rubbish or writing lines. It meant running through a forest in the middle of the night with dogs chasing you. Or being locked in a room with something terrifying, something blood-curdling, something hideously ugly. And it wasn't Stenka.

But there was something else about Monstrum House that was different to other schools. It had something no other school had ever had.

Excitement.

Hunting monsters was *exciting*. And *that* is what gave Jasper a buzz.

Jasper was staring at a fly.

He still couldn't get the fishy taste out of his mouth. His friend Felix had suggested rubbing his mouth out with soap – but all that'd done was make him throw up. His friend Saffy told him never to feel sorry for a monster again.

Some friends, thought Jasper.

Mr Golag, the Mental Manipulations teacher, was lurching up and down between the desks. He was a hairy, thick-set man with a hunched back and a lumpy face.

'*Be* the fly,' he wheezed. 'From understanding comes control.'

Everyone sat silently at their desks, staring intently at the flies trapped under the glass jars in front of them.

The classroom was gloomy. It was only lit by lamps, as Mr Golag didn't like bright lights.

At one time Jasper would have thought that spending a whole class sitting in a dimly lit room staring at flies was boring, but not now. After months of nothing but reading and theory, Mental Manipulations class looked as though it was finally about to get interesting.

Jasper knew that of all his classes, Mental Manipulations could turn out to be the most important. Although they were only starting off with flies, by third year they would be learning how to mentally manipulate monsters, and *that* would be seriously cool.

Mental manipulation was how the teachers trained the monsters that were used in student tests. It didn't work on all monsters, and it didn't always work as planned, but Jasper figured that being able to influence a monster into not eating him would be a definite advantage.

'Watch,' said Mr Golag. He pointed to a large sack hanging from the roof. 'Inside that sack,' he continued quietly, 'is a Cranklesucker.'

Mr Golag untied the sack and carried it gently to the front of the class. He smiled and lay the sack fondly by his feet.

Cool, Jasper thought, as a forked claw silently reached out of the opening in the sack.

'Cranklesuckers belong to the Muncher order of monsters,' said Mr Golag.

OK, maybe not quite so cool, thought Jasper. He wasn't so sure he liked being in the same room as a Muncher. Even a trained one.

Cranklesucker
DANGER!
Don't get too close, it sucks!
Species: Cranklesucker
Order: Muncher

A look of concentration came over Mr Golag's face, and then he whistled a command. There was a moment of tense silence, and then the sack opened wide. The Cranklesucker scuttled out of the sack and skidded around the students before coming and sitting obediently at Mr Golag's feet.

Jasper didn't think the Cranklesucker seemed too bad, for a monster. It looked like some sort of bat-dog. Well, a warped bat-dog, with venomous lumpy spines and big fangs.

'A Cranklesucker is a bit like a leech in monster form,' Mr Golag announced. 'It may not look so dangerous, but in the wild, this little beauty will latch onto your nose and suck you dry of blood in four minutes and twenty-eight seconds.'

Jasper felt himself move back in his chair. The monster had turned around and seemed to be eyeballing the students one by one.

Probably working out which of us is the juiciest, Jasper thought.

'But don't Munchers *eat* people?' asked Saffy, apparently not worried that there was a blood-sucking killer in the room. 'Is it still a Muncher if it sucks your blood?'

'Munchers don't always eat whole people,' said Mr Golag. 'Many of them just eat parts of people. And your blood is a part of you.'

'Oh, that's much better,' muttered Felix.

'In fact, Cranklesuckers don't even use their teeth to attack. They use their lips for suction. But don't worry,' Mr Golag continued. 'I have this Cranklesucker so perfectly trained that he won't even think about the delicious, salty-sweet young blood in the room. At least, not while I keep focused on exactly what I want him to do.'

Mr Golag went quiet again. Jasper got the feeling that his teacher knew just a bit too much about how young blood might taste. It wasn't a comforting thought.

Mr Golag must have noticed the way Jasper was looking at him. 'Ahem. It's all about getting into the right frame of mind,' he explained. 'You must *think* like the creature you are manipulating.'

Then Mr Golag whistled once again, and this time the monster scurried up his leg and around his back, before perching happily on his head. Mr Golag smiled, and looked around the class as though expecting applause.

'There. So simple. Just focus.' Mr Golag gestured back at the flies in their glass jars. 'Focus, and *think* like a fly.'

Jasper was still trying to work out exactly how a fly might think, when he felt Mr Golag's hairy, knobbly hand on his shoulder.

'Good. First *think*, then *do*!' he whispered in Jasper's ear.

Jasper looked at the fly. He imagined he *was* the fly, swooping towards the top of the glass. He thought about the sensation of taking off into the air.

'Yes!' Mr Golag cheered as Jasper's fly took off inside the glass. Jasper was sure it had been a fluke, but he wasn't about to say so.

Mr Golag thumped Jasper's shoulder in encouragement, before heaving his way back to the front of the classroom.

Jasper tested his fly again, imagining how it would feel to circle around the glass, and then land on his head. Sure enough, the fly flew three perfect circles around the glass, then settled into a perfect fly headstand.

Awesome, Jasper thought. He grinned and

started fantasising about the pranks he'd play if he could control something – even a fly.

Jasper glanced up at Mr Golag. The teacher was rummaging around in the sack, mumbling as he did so. The Cranklesucker had moved onto Mr Golag's shoulder and was bobbing happily up and down, humming to itself.

Jasper lifted the glass away from the fly. But rather than buzzing off, the fly stayed on the desk, looking at him.

Jasper stared closely at the fly. He imagined his legs pushing off from the table top, zooming up into the air, his wings buzzing merrily as he made his way towards Saffy who was sitting three desks away.

Watch out, Saffy, here I come, Jasper thought.

Jasper couldn't believe it. The fly did exactly as he had thought. It headed directly for Saffy, took a left turn at her desk, and shot straight up her nose.

'Urgh!' Saffy yelled.

She jumped from her desk, knocking her own glass to the floor as she flung her arms around. She sneezed violently, sending Jasper's fly spinning out of control across the room. She sneezed again and stumbled backwards, toppling more jars to the floor.

Mr Golag was moving towards Saffy when he tripped over a power cord that had been covered by the Cranklesucker's sack. The lamps in the room all went out and there was a sickening thud as Mr Golag's head smashed against the corner of a chair. He wobbled to his feet again, but didn't get far.

'I ...' he muttered, then collapsed in a crumpled heap on the floor.

Uh-oh, thought Jasper.

No-one moved. Except the Cranklesucker.

It jumped from Mr Golag's shoulder onto the desk. Jasper could just make out its black rubbery lips in the darkness.

The Cranklesucker lifted its front feet off the desk, surveying the students. Jasper felt as though he was caught in a scene from some nature documentary – and he wasn't the lion. Then the room went cold.

'I guess Mr Golag's not so focused now,' Jasper whispered.

'Someone get the lights!' Jasper heard Felix call from the front of the room.

The Cranklesucker tilted its head towards Felix. And then it pounced.

Felix's scream was instantly muffled as the Cranklesucker suctioned onto his nose. Jasper leapt from his seat and tried to grab the monster from behind, but its lumpy spines made it hard to get a hold of.

Someone had managed to plug the cord for the lamps back in, but it didn't help. The Cranklesucker was latched onto Felix and getting bigger, its body swelling with blood.

Felix was out cold and his skin had turned blue. All that could be heard was the horrible sucking of the monster. There wasn't much time left.

'Wake up Mr Golag,' cried Saffy, slapping the teacher in the face.

He didn't respond.

'We need water,' yelled Saffy, and ran out of the classroom.

Ten minutes later, Jasper was standing in front of Mr Golag's desk. He was in shock. He still couldn't believe that he had gotten Felix Monstered, *again*.

It was lucky that Saffy had managed to get a jug of cold water and throw it over Mr Golag – the Cranklesucker only managed one minute and ten seconds worth of suction before Mr Golag was conscious enough to take back control.

Felix had been rushed to the hospital wing

for an emergency blood transfusion.

Jasper was trying very hard not to think about the punishment Mr Golag was going to dish out. But he knew that whatever it was, he deserved it. *More* than deserved it.

Mr Golag sat silently. He hadn't said anything for ten minutes. He kept tugging at the bandage wrapped around his head and sighing.

'Do you think the fly *enjoyed* its journey up Ms Dominguez's nose?' Mr Golag asked finally.

Jasper shook his head. He hadn't exactly been thinking about the fly.

'Exactly,' Mr Golag replied. 'You must *always* think about your subjects. If you are going to manipulate someone's mind, you must *always* do it from the highest moral ground. Otherwise you are no better than the creatures we are training you to catch.'

Jasper couldn't bring himself to reply.

I'm sorry didn't seem to cover it. He wondered how he was going to make it up to Felix.

'I am so very disappointed in you,' Mr Golag said sadly, shaking his head. 'Dismissed.'

Jasper froze. He had been expecting some serious penalty points. But Mr Golag simply looked towards the door.

Slowly, Jasper turned and left the classroom. It was weird – he hadn't been punished, but he wished that he had. The guilt he was feeling was far worse than any punishment.

'Oi!' came a deep voice.

Jasper stopped. *Oh, great*, he thought. *The thug brigade*.

A prefect stood blocking the doorway, his black camouflage and slicked-back hair marking him out from the other students in their coloured hoodies and tracksuit pants.

'You should be in class,' the prefect snarled.

'Thanks, Bruno. That's where I'm *trying* to go,' said Jasper.

Jasper had already had a few run-ins with Bruno, the head prefect.

Prefects at Monstrum House had the authority to dish out punishments, and they liked to make life as painful as possible for everyone.

They were different from the other students. They didn't go to monster-hunting classes or sleep in the sleep halls, or eat meals at the same time as everyone else. In fact, they didn't even know monsters existed. But Jasper wasn't sure whether this was because they were too old to see them or too dumb to realise what was really going on at Monstum House.

'You're already on fourteen penalty points,

aren't you, McPhee?' Bruno snarled. Jasper didn't answer. One thing the prefects did know was exactly how many penalty points each student was on. 'Well, I reckon an extra six for being out of class should do it.'

Jasper shrugged.

'Which brings you up to, hmmm, let me see ...' Bruno pretended to be working it out as he wrote something down on a card. 'Oh no, twenty penalty points. Looks like you've got yourself a punishment. Enjoy.'

Bruno slapped Jasper in the face with a red card before strutting down the corridor.

Jasper looked down at the card. There was the school emblem, Bruno's ugly signature, and the words:

MkFee. ABEENT ABSINT
NOT iN cLASS. 6 POiNTS.
20 POiNTS TOTAL. PUNeSHMUNT.

Jasper stifled a groan. Once you reached twenty penalty points, that was it – punishment time. The punishment changed each day, and was written up by Stenka on the punishment board, as if it was a special at a restaurant. *This day just keeps getting better,* Jasper thought.

He scuffed his way to the board. The words

PENALTY COURSE

were neatly written in chalk. He let out a sigh of relief. Jasper had run the penalty course before, so at least he knew what to expect. It could have been worse. Much worse. Stenka must be in a good mood today.

Not that the penalty course was a whole lot of fun. It went straight through the middle of the forest. Running through a cold forest was hard enough during the day. But in the dead of night, when who knew *what* monsters lurked there – that was definitely creepy.

Kids said that years ago, some of the trained monsters had turned feral and escaped, retreating to the dark depths of the trees. So far Jasper hadn't seen anything to confirm this, but it was hard not to think about it when you were running through the forest at night.

Of course, the guard dogs usually helped to take his mind off the monsters. Ten minutes after the students started running, a pack of guard dogs was released to chase them. Jasper figured that guard-dog teeth would hurt just as much as monster teeth.

The gong sounded for the end of class, startling Jasper. Between talking to Mr Golag, running into Bruno and checking the board, he had managed to miss his Species Studies class with Stenka.

He could just imagine her smile. Stenka had a smile straight out of a horror film. She flashed it when the students were about to go through something unpleasant. And then there were her cold, beady eyes that shot straight into your soul. Jasper felt the hair on his arms bristle.

He really hoped she hadn't noticed that he wasn't in class. But Stenka *always* noticed.

'Come on – it will be fun!' Saffy was saying to Felix as they made their way through the study hall towards Jasper.

Felix had been let out of hospital, but he was still looking very pale. Jasper had gone to visit him earlier that afternoon, but the nurses wouldn't let him in.

Jasper was supposed to be catching up on the Species Studies class he'd missed, but for the last half-hour he'd found himself drawing a picture of Felix being sucked by the Cranklesucker. It was hard to get it out of his mind.

As Felix and Saffy came over, Jasper quickly closed his exercise book.

'Hey, Felix,' he said quietly. He noticed Felix had a big bruise on his face from where the Cranklesucker had latched on.

Saffy gave Jasper a particularly vicious glare. 'Just try something like that fly stunt again,' she threatened, 'and your puny little backside will be on the wrong end of my foot.'

Jasper didn't argue – Saffy was a kickboxing champion.

Felix gave Jasper a small smile. 'Don't worry about it. I mean, that monster was ...' he shuddered. 'But it's not as though you set it on me. And anyway, now I can brag to my brothers about how I survived a Muncher attack.'

Jasper breathed a sigh of relief.

'Well, we can't afford to stay annoyed with

you for too long,' said Saffy, brightening. 'You'll never guess why.'

'Um, because I'm so funny and cool?' tried Jasper.

'Yeah, right,' said Saffy. 'We've got to stick together because we're all on the same team.'

'What are you talking about?' asked Jasper.

Felix frowned. 'Our first Task.'

Jasper sat up straighter in his chair. 'Already? A Task?'

'Yup. Stenka told us in Species Studies,' said Saffy. You're in so much trouble for missing her class, by the way. We've all been teamed up together. Look out monsters, here we come!'

'I think I've had enough of monsters for one day,' muttered Felix.

'Come on, Felix!' said Saffy. 'This is our big chance!' Her eyes shone with excitement.

A Task was the first big step towards going

on a real Hunt. It was a practice Hunt, in the school grounds.

Jasper was desperate to go on a Hunt. It would be his first chance to catch wild monsters in the outside world. He imagined himself saving people from the Screechers that were lurking under their beds, the Morphers that were changing them into other things, the Scramblers that were driving them crazy, and the Munchers who wanted to eat them ... or suck their faces off.

'Listen,' said Saffy. 'Once we pass our Task, we'll be that much closer to going on a real Hunt. And do you know what the best thing about that is?' She lowered her voice. 'If we go on a Hunt, we'll be out of this dump! There'll be no teachers, no more thug brigade, no more monsters trying to suck us to death. We'll be free to nick off wherever we want.'

'Where would we go?' asked Felix. 'We don't even know where we are.'

'Who cares?' said Saffy. 'Anywhere!'

Jasper could see Felix's point. They really had no idea where they were. But he still wanted to go on a Hunt. Only students went on Hunts – no teachers, no prefects.

Jasper thought about the buzz he got from catching the Quiddlesquawk in his test. If it felt that good catching a trained monster, how great would it be to catch a wild one? That is, if it didn't catch him first.

'It's going to be awesome,' said Saffy. 'Don't you want to get out of here, Felix? This is our ticket out!'

Felix rolled his eyes. Jasper wondered if he was thinking about their first escape attempt.

Saffy had been trying to escape ever since she got to Monstrum House. Her nickname was

Houdini. She had escaped from every boarding school her parents had ever dumped her in.

'OK, whatever, but get this,' said Saffy, 'the first team to catch the monster and bring it back gets the reward of not having to run the penalty course through the forest for six nights in a row.'

'Yeah, meaning if you *don't* catch the monster you *do* have to run the course,' said Felix.

'Don't worry,' said Jasper. 'We'll catch the monster in no time. We're an awesome team.'

Felix sighed. 'I don't even know why I'm at this school. You both seem to kind of enjoy catching monsters, but I would much rather be at home, even with my brothers thumping me. I mean,' he dropped his voice to a whisper, 'what if it's, like, a dangerous monster?'

'Come on, you're an expert at karate, remember?' said Jasper.

'That's only for self-defence,' protested Felix. 'And anyway, these monsters are brutal. Look!' he said, pointing to the textbook that lay open in front of Jasper.

Jasper glanced at the book on his desk. The *Big Book of Beastly Behaviour: Level One.* The book lay open to a picture of a monster stalking a small girl. The monster's mouth was open wide, and it looked as though it was just seconds away from chomping down on the child.

A Beastly book →

Jasper had to admit that Felix had a point. And he had a massive bruise on his face to prove it.

'Are you sure you're OK?' asked Jasper.

'Yeah. It wasn't that bad in hospital,' said Felix. 'The nurse gave me chocolate all day to raise my blood-sugar levels. *And* I get out of doing the monthly test. It was just bad luck,' he said. 'It wasn't really your fault.'

'Well, it was, actually,' said Saffy. 'If you hadn't sent that fly up my nose ... But we've got bigger things to worry about now.'

Jasper was relieved. But he knew Saffy was right.

Somewhere in the school grounds, the teachers were letting a monster loose. He hoped it was trained not to do any real damage.

But at Monstrum House it was best not to assume anything.

Jasper and Saffy stood outside in the cold, huddled under a security light. 'You're sure this is where Stenka said to wait for instructions?' Jasper asked again.

Saffy nodded and peered into the dark. 'The Task starts tomorrow, but the clue for our Task-team is supposed to be delivered at 9.30pm, outside Light Tower 2.'

Jasper checked the time on his watch. It was 9.28pm. 'Felix better hurry,' he muttered,

stamping his feet. He didn't think the clue was likely to be late.

As if on cue, Felix stumbled through the door and into the cold. 'Sorry,' he puffed, the steam from his breath rising into the icy air. 'I didn't miss anything, did I?'

Jasper and Saffy shook their heads.

'9.29,' Jasper murmured anxiously.

There was silence as they stood in the dark. Jasper edged closer to the wall, making sure nothing could sneak up on him from behind. He had a feeling that the clue would not ·be pleasant.

'Ten, nine, eight ...' Jasper started counting down in time with his watch.

'Shhh,' said Saffy.

'What?' Jasper asked. 'Don't you want to know how much longer –'

There was a crunch in the snow. They all

froze, hardly daring to breathe. Jasper wondered if the clue would hurt – or, more exactly, how *much* the clue would hurt.

It didn't take long for him to find out.

A sharp pain hit Jasper's shoulder as something bounced off it and into the snow. It looked like a rock covered in paper.

Saffy looked relieved. 'I'm glad they aimed at you rather than – Ow!' she yelped, as a rock bounced off her leg.

Jasper couldn't help but smile.

Another rock hit Felix square in the back, despite his attempt to hide behind Saffy.

A snigger of satisfaction was heard from the darkness. Jasper wasn't surprised to see a prefect through the beam of the security light. The prefect sneered and waved a slingshot at them as he passed by.

'What's wrong with *handing* us a note?'

Jasper asked.

Felix elbowed him in the ribs. 'Shh, would you?' he hissed. 'Don't provoke the thugs.'

The prefect vanished back into the darkness. Jasper figured he had moved on to deliver more notes. He reached down and picked up his rock.

He read his note out loud: 'In the darkness underground, I creep and crawl without a sound.'

Saffy read her note: 'If you hunt me, best beware, I am nastiest at my lair.'

Saffy and Jasper looked at Felix.

'Oh, right,' he said, unwrapping his rock and reading. 'But just a single button pressed will send me to a lengthy rest.'

Jasper re-read the notes carefully. 'That's the clue? That's all the help we get?'

It didn't make sense. Saffy looked stumped

In the darkness
underground,
I creep and crawl
without a sound

If you hunt me,
best beware —
I am nastiest at my lair

But just a single button
pressed
Will send me to a
lengthy rest.

as well. But Felix was staring off into the night, with a look of concentration on his face.

'Hang on a minute,' said Felix. 'I know this.' He was clicking his fingers. 'I've heard it before.'

Jasper and Saffy looked at him curiously.

'It's a Grubbergrind.'

'A Grubberwhat?' asked Saffy, looking confused.

'A Grubbergrind,' Felix repeated confidently. 'That's the answer. I've just saved us a night of study.' He looked particularly pleased with himself.

'But how do you ... What makes you so sure?' asked Jasper.

'It's from this poem I heard ages ago,' said Felix. 'When I was about five, my brothers came home from school for the holidays. They were trying to scare me about this thing called a Grubbergrind. They had this poem about it. It was the same as the clues we were just given, but it had an extra line:

In the darkness underground, I creep and crawl without a sound.
If you hunt me best beware, I am nastiest at my lair.
But just a single button pressed will send me to a lengthy rest.
There's one thing you won't care to find: the eight legs of the Grubbergrind.

'My brothers would chase me, pretending to be a Grubbergrind that was going to eat me. I thought it was just something they'd made up. I didn't think it really existed!'

'Well, it must,' said Saffy. 'And we're going to catch it. Felix, you are so cool!'

Felix blushed.

'So, a Grubber ... grind,' said Jasper. 'And your brothers said it was going to eat you. It's a Muncher, isn't it?' He gulped. After what had happened in Mental Manipulations, Jasper didn't want anything to do with another Muncher.

Felix shugged unhappily. 'I guess so. The *grind* part does makes it sound like a Muncher.'

Saffy was still shaking her head in disbelief. 'I can't believe you can remember something like a weird poem from so long ago.'

'I remember all kinds of stuff like that,' said Felix. 'Especially about monsters.' He shuddered.

'Awesome,' said Saffy. 'So where do we find this Grubbythingy?'

'I don't know,' said Felix. 'I only know the poem. I've got no idea what it looks like or where to find it, so I reckon we'd all better get ready to run the penalty course for the next week anyway.'

'That reminds me,' said Jasper. 'I've got to run the penalty course tonight. I'd better go.'

'Watch out for the Grubbywhatsy,' Saffy called after him cheerfully. 'They might've already released it.'

'That's not funny,' said Felix, pulling out his asthma puffer. 'Um, can we go back now? I mean, I did nearly die today.'

Jasper trudged along the icy ground towards the edge of the forest. The further away from the school building he was, the more the darkness grew around him. The clue for the Task kept beating through his head. *In the darkness underground, I creep and crawl without a sound ...*

He wondered if the monster for the Task *had* already been released into the school grounds. Who knew what was creeping and crawling without a sound around him?

Jasper entered the forest, heading towards

the lantern that hung from a tree branch, illuminating the starting point for the penalty course.

There were three boys and two girls from other year levels waiting to begin the penalty course. Jasper recognised one of the older boys as Mac, who sat at his table in the food hall. Mac was a hunt captain, and he seemed to love Monstrum House. He was one of the best monster-hunters in the school, and Jasper didn't want to let on how much the forest gave him the creeps.

'Hey, Jasp,' said Mac. 'What's your best time on the penalty course? I reckon I'll beat you hands down. You all right? You're looking a bit nervous. Don't worry, you'll be tucked up in bed before you know it.'

Sometimes Mac could be just a little bit annoying.

Jasper was about to reply when a dog's harsh bark cracked through the night and a tall, thin, man stepped from the shadows.

Jasper wondered how long he had been standing there. His body seemed to hunch and twist around like a gnarled old tree. It was the perfect camouflage.

'Good evening,' the man said calmly.

'Good evening, Mondrag,' they replied.

Mondrag was the guard dog trainer and in charge of the penalty course. Behind him, two vicious-looking guard dogs strained on their leads. They looked like German shepherds crossed with wolf hounds or something. They were huge. Jasper took an involuntary step backwards.

'The hounds will be released in ten minutes,' said Mondrag. 'I suggest that you start running now.'

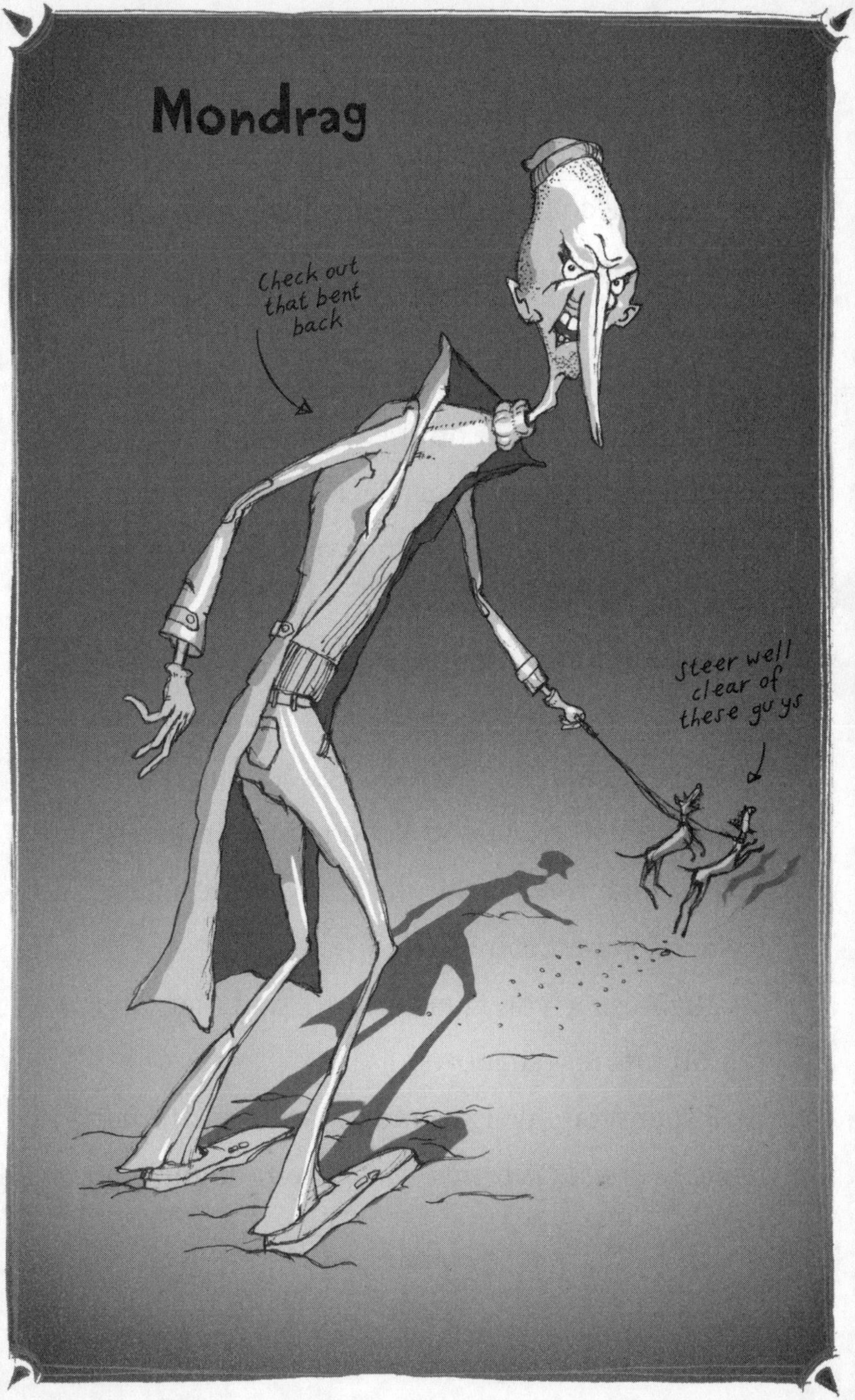
Mondrag
Check out that bent back
Steer well clear of these guys

Jasper tried not to think of the dogs' sharp teeth as he followed the other kids along the path through the trees.

Jasper was a strong runner and the penalty course wasn't particularly long, but tonight it felt like his feet were on the wrong legs. He was tripping up all over the place. He caught his foot on a tree root as he ran, and went flying head-first into the undergrowth.

'Are you OK?' Mac stopped to help Jasper up.

Jasper nodded. 'Thanks. I've lost my shoe, but it's no worries, you keep going. Seriously, I'll overtake you in a minute anyway,' he added, trying to sound confident.

'Righto, see you later, speedy,' said Mac, and ran off into the shadows.

Jasper scrambled around in the dark. *My shoe has to be around here somewhere*, he thought.

He stooped under a branch and felt a spiderweb cling to his face. He wiped his face frantically and stumbled backwards, tripping over his shoe in his panic.

He took a deep breath and forced himself to calm down. He knew that being scared of spiders was stupid, but they still got to him. Just the thought of their black eyes, their hairy legs, the way they scuttled … it gave him the creeps.

Jasper jammed his shoe on and took off after the others. All he could hear were his own footsteps cracking over the frozen ground.

The words of the Task clue ran through Jasper's mind again. *I creep and crawl without a sound*. He tried to push the thought away, but it was too late. *The Grubbergrind could be out here right now.* If the poem was right, he would never hear it – not until it was too late.

He couldn't see Mac or the other kids

anywhere. He guessed they would be reaching the school soon and crawling back into bed.

Jasper had run this course before, but he had never been quite so creeped out. He tried to run even faster, but stumbled and tripped again. Then he froze to the spot. He suddenly knew that something was there, watching him.

And he hadn't heard a thing.

7

Jasper turned around slowly. Snow had begun to fall, and moonlight shone down. And what Jasper saw in the moonlight made his breath catch in his throat.

A guard dog stood directly in front of him. It wasn't a monster, but still, this dog looked nasty. It let out a fierce, low growl, and Jasper's heart leapt in his chest. The dog was huge, with sharp, gleaming teeth. Jasper wasn't scared of dogs, but this one looked, well, vicious. It was a trained guard dog, and what it was probably trained to do was ferociously rip you to pieces.

Dogs can sense fear, Jasper told himself. He didn't like his chances in a one-on-one fight. He looked at the trees – but he knew he could never climb one in time. The dog would get to him first.

Jasper took a deep breath and crouched down, his hand held out towards the dog. He tried to treat it like a friendly puppy. 'Hiya, pup,' he said as calmly as he could.

The dog growled more loudly, its teeth still bared.

Jasper held his breath. He had a bad feeling he was about to get torn apart. 'Good dog?' Jasper said hopefully. He tried to imagine it was one of his dogs at home, but they were both fat labradors. It wasn't quite the same.

The dog snapped its jaws shut and cocked its head to one side. It seemed to be deciding

Mondrag's guard dog

whether or not to bite him.

'Not,' Jasper whispered.

The dog sat down and whined at Jasper, licking his outstretched hand. Jasper slowly let his breath out and gave the dog a pat.

'You *are* a good dog, aren't you, fella?' Jasper murmured as he rubbed the dog's head.

It was so nice to encounter something that was *friendly*. Jasper suddenly felt homesick. He missed creatures that didn't want to eat him. He missed his dogs. He missed good food. He missed his bedroom, with the walls covered in comics he'd drawn. He missed his cosy bed. He missed his mum. He even missed his sisters.

He had been writing letters home to his mum every couple of weeks as promised. Each letter was more of a lie than the last. When she dropped him off at Monstrum House she had told him to be careful – but she had no idea just how hard that was in a school crawling with monsters.

Jasper didn't like lying to his mum, but he also didn't want her to worry about him. What good would come of telling her about being shoved in monster-infested rooms or being made to stand in the snow for hours? Would she even believe him?

Jasper wanted to make his mum proud. If he could just make it through his first year without being expelled, he knew she'd be happy.

The funny thing was, Jasper wasn't such a bad student at this school. He was actually OK at the classes. In a funny way, Monstrum House suited him – the stuff they learnt came easily to him. It just made more sense than normal school.

'I bet Mondrag doesn't pat you much, does he, fella?' Jasper asked, as the dog rubbed its muzzle against him. He ruffled the dog's ears, then gently pushed it away.

He sighed and got up. 'I still have ages to go through this course,' he muttered. 'And chances are the thug brigade are already on the prowl, waiting to catch me out of bed and give me more penalty points.'

Jasper was about to start his run along the path through the forest again, when the dog barked sharply. Jasper stopped and turned. The dog barked again, and gripped the bottom of Jasper's hoodie firmly in its mouth.

The dog pulled at it, wrenching Jasper away from the path. Jasper resisted. He wasn't sure this was such a good idea. How did he know where the dog would take him? After all, it *had* been trained by Mondrag. What if it was a trap?

But there were no rules to say you had to run the penalty course along the path, it's just what everyone did. Perhaps there was another way through the forest.

The dog barked again, and Jasper realised he didn't have much of a choice. He didn't want to argue with those teeth.

'OK, OK,' Jasper gave in, and followed the dog into the trees, away from the well-worn track.

It was darker and denser in the forest than Jasper had thought possible, and he could hear strange noises.

But before he had a chance to be worried he was suddenly back at the school. The dog had just saved him half an hour! He couldn't believe it – they had come out from the forest almost directly next to the mansion. Jasper didn't even know the forest stretched this close – and he had made it his mission to know his way around the campus.

Searchlights flashed around the school grounds, but the Monstrum House mansion loomed large and dark above them, casting a shadow over Jasper. The dog led Jasper through a hole in the fence, and right up to the school. It gave him a gentle nudge and scratched at the wall. Jasper scraped away the dead ivy to find a small door.

'You're serious?' he asked. The dog just stared at him. 'Well, you got me here – I guess I'll take your word for it. Thanks.' Jasper gave the dog a final pat. He checked the name on its tag:

WOOF

'Hmmm, original name.' Woof licked Jasper's hand before slinking silently back into the shadows of the forest.

Jasper twisted the handle of the door and grimaced as it gave a loud squeak. He waited for a prefect's hand to land on him, but nothing happened. Jasper carefully pulled open the door. There was a dark tunnel ahead of him. He knew that once he closed the door behind him, he would be in darkness. He took a deep breath and climbed inside.

Jasper felt his way along the tunnel. It was a tight squeeze, and he had to commando-crawl along on his stomach, pushing his feet against the sides of the tunnel. Every now and then, the tunnel would stop and turn upwards, and he would have to squirm into a sitting position so he could haul himself up a ladder. He wondered what the tunnel was for. Where did it go?

The tunnel kept rising, until Jasper was sure he was up at least one storey high. Every now and then he could hear kids' whispers as he crawled along. *I must be passing by the sleep halls,* he thought.

'OOOOOOHHHHHH,' he moaned, hoping to give the kids in the hall a fright. There was a muffled squeal, and then silence. Jasper grinned. He hoped that was Saffy he'd frightened.

Then Jasper started to hear a different kind of whispering. A spooky kind of whispering. It didn't sound like kids. It didn't sound *human*. It seemed to seep from the walls. *Craaag ... kroomt ... lisss ... en ... lissssen ... Jaaaaasssssper.*

Jasper had heard this whispering before. He'd heard it when he first stepped off the plane to Monstrum House. And he'd heard it again in the maze of corridors near the records office.

Jasper moved quickly along the tunnel, trying to get away from the eerie whispering. But it seemed to be growing. It filled every bit of the tunnel. Was it telling him to *listen?*

Jasper came to another ladder and climbed it as quickly as he could. Where would the tunnel end?

There must at least be some air vents or something, he thought. He felt along the wall with his fingers. Nothing. Jasper climbed another ladder, this time running one hand along the wall, feeling for something – anything – that might indicate a way out.

He had just begun to crawl along the passage again when his hand hit a bolt on the bottom of the tunnel. He could feel a large panel around it. The bolt was rusty, but after some frantic jiggling, it came loose.

He gently eased the panel open and found himself staring down from the ceiling of a dimly lit bathroom.

Jasper had used this bathroom before, but he'd never noticed the small hatch in the ceiling.

He listened carefully for danger, his every sense working overtime.

But the whispering had stopped.

Jasper's heart slowed. He shook the fear from his body. *Get a grip,* he told himself.

He was about to jump down from the hatch when he heard the door to the bathroom creak open. He froze. *Who's using these toilets in the middle of the night?* he wondered. They were nowhere near the sleep halls.

The lights flashed on and Mr Golag appeared, hauling a large sack into the bathroom.

Jasper didn't have enough time to pull the hatch shut. He just hoped that Mr Golag didn't look up. Jasper hardly dared to breathe.

'Nearly there,' Mr Golag panted. He puffed heavily as he swung the sack off his shoulder and gently pulled it open. Jasper caught sight of something a bit like an octopus, with slimy grey tentacles that had razor-sharp nippers on the ends. Mr Golag smiled lovingly and patted its wart-covered head, before up-ending the sack and dropping the monster into the toilet with a splash.

'There you go, my beauty,' Mr Golag cooed to the creature and dropped a leg of chicken into the toilet. There was the sound of mad splashing as the monster devoured the meat. Then Mr Golag pressed the flush button and the monster disappeared with a splash. 'Awww,' Mr Golag clucked, and slunk quietly out of the bathroom, turning off the light as he went.

Jasper had no idea what to do. Could the monster get out of the toilet? He racked his brain, trying to remember if Stenka had ever told them anything about toilet-dwelling monsters during their Species Studies classes. All the monsters he'd learnt about seemed to

Mr Golag's pet

have flown from his head, leaving him with nothing.

'There is no way I am ever using that toilet again,' Jasper mumbled to himself.

In fact, how could Jasper ever use *any* toilet? The toilets were all connected by pipes – the monster could be in any one of them, just waiting to nip some poor unsuspecting student.

Jasper couldn't hear splashing coming from the toilet. *It's now or never*, he told himself. He took a deep breath and leapt from the hatch, aiming as far away from the toilets as possible. He landed softly and was out the bathroom door before he even had a chance to catch his breath.

What on earth is Mr Golag doing letting a beast like that loose in the school? Jasper thought.

And then it struck him. *The Task!*

9

and typed something. Felix was about to

Stenka looked at the students. She was smiling.
This couldn't be good.

'Your first Task,' she beamed.

Despite Stenka's threatening smile, Jasper
was feeling pretty pleased. He hadn't told Saffy
and Felix about his discovery the night before –
he was saving that for after class.

'A simple exercise really,' Stenka continued,
walking up and down between the couches in
the Species Studies class. This classroom was
the best in Monstrum House, with cosy couches

and an open fireplace. But it wasn't enough to take the chill off Stenka's smile.

'You have twenty-four hours to catch the monster. You had all night to research your clue. I imagine most of you have some idea of the monster you will be hunting?' Stenka looked around at the room of students. Nobody seemed confident. But then no-one else had the inside information that Jasper, Felix and Saffy had!

Jasper glanced down at their collection of clues!

In the darkness underground, I creep and crawl without a sound.

If you hunt me, best beware, I am nastiest at my lair.

But just a single button pressed will send me to a lengthy rest.

The secret last line ran through his head. *There's one thing you won't care to find: the eight legs of the Grubbergrind.*

They were going to nail this Task.

Stenka rapped her stick down in front of Saffy. 'Well? Let's hear it, Ms Dominguez. What kind of monster are you trying to catch?'

Saffy blinked. 'Um,' she stammered. 'We know. It's a Grubby ... a Grubbo ... '

Felix was trying to mouth the word 'Grubbergrind' to Saffy without Stenka seeing. But Stenka always saw.

She cuffed Felix over the back of the head. 'I don't believe your name is Ms Dominguez, now is it, Mr Brown?' she hissed. Felix gulped and shut his mouth. 'Well?' Stenka turned back to Saffy.

'Um ... an underground kind of monster?' Saffy mumbled feebly.

Stenka handed Saffy a card with two penalty points on it.

Jasper thought that, technically, Saffy was right. He debated pointing this out to Stenka, but the look on her face told him not to.

'And while I'm handing out points,' said Stenka, 'Don't *ever* miss my class again.' She handed Jasper a card with four penalty points on it.

Stenka turned back to Saffy. 'Now, Ms Dominguez, can you at least give me the monster's order?'

'Um … we think it's a Muncher.'

There were uneasy mumurs from the rest of the class.

'Think? Or know?' asked Stenka.

Saffy shrugged.

Stenka stopped smiling. 'Lucky guess,' she barked. 'But I would advise you to learn your monster names, Ms Dominguez. And most particularly their weaknesses.'

It *was* a Muncher. There was silence in the room as the realisation sunk in.

'Couldn't they have chosen something less, well, dangerous?' Felix muttered.

Jasper had to agree. After all, lots of monsters didn't actually kill people, they just … messed with them a bit.

'Now,' said Stenka, turning to the class. 'You are free to take any supplies from Storeroom A for the Task. You should find everything you need in there.'

Supplies! This Task was starting to sound better. Jasper wondered if they'd finally discover that this school was packed with cool monster-catching gadgets. Maybe there would be something like Spiderman web-shooters! He sketched himself in the back of his textbook, shooting a web over the squelchy toilet monster as he flew through the air.

'Fancy yourself a spider-man, Mr McPhee?' Stenka asked, raising an eyebrow.

Jasper quickly covered up his sketch.

'You should know that you may get injured during the Task,' Stenka said sternly to the class. It was almost as though the teachers thought that real learning only took place through pain. 'This is a monster you are hunting. While we have trained the beast as much as possible, it is still a monster with monstrous instincts.'

Jasper thought of all the monsters he had met. He looked down at the textbook in front of him and felt his heart race a little. *Still, the Grubbergrind didn't seem so vicious in the bathroom*, he thought.

'The trained monsters we use in Tasks are much less dangerous than the wild monsters

The Species studies text book

-8 26 8-

-8 27 8-

Gulp, not that again.

you will encounter on a Hunt outside the school. But the monster will do all it can to stop itself being caught and, at the same time, attempt to capture and eat you,' said Stenka.

Felix was beginning to look queasy. Even his bruises were taking on a green tinge.

'The Task is intended to test those characteristics you need to become skilled monster-hunters,' Stenka continued, ignoring the mumbled complaints from the class. 'To catch the Grubbergrind before it catches you, you must know it's weakness. What is the weakness of a Grubbergrind, Mr Brown?'

'Something to do with a button?' said Felix. Jasper couldn't wait to tell Felix what the button clue was about.

'Yes, well that *was* the clue,' said Stenka. 'This Task is a privilege. A chance to prove yourselves. Please indulge us by at least *trying*

to use your rapidly shrinking brains.'

'A privilege?' Felix muttered. 'Except for the lucky team of kids who manage to actually catch the monster, the rest of us will be caught, hurt, possibly eaten, and then punished by the teachers for not catching the stupid thing. This is really, *really* bad.'

Jasper didn't bother telling Felix that it'd be hard for the teachers to punish you if you'd already been eaten.

By the time the gong sounded for the end of the class, there weren't many people who were still excited about the Task – except for Jasper. Even though he knew the monster could eat him, he figured his chances of survival were pretty good. Knowing that the monster was in the bathroom pipes was a huge advantage for his team.

Stenka rapped a stick against her desk.

'I don't remember dismissing this class.' Everyone fell silent. 'Your Task has begun,' she said quietly. 'Good luck.'

Everyone froze. Did they actually hear her say *good luck*? Perhaps she was talking to the monster.

Felix peered into the toilet bowl. 'In there?' he asked for the third time. 'I used that toilet this morning,' he said.

'I've been peeing out the window,' Jasper admitted.

Saffy threw him a disgusted look.

'So, what do you think?' Jasper asked.

Neither Saffy or Felix looked very sure.

'Listen,' said Jasper. 'I've been thinking it through all night. We have a massive head start. We know what it is and where it is. The other kids will still be trying to figure out how to catch it. From what I saw last night, all we need is a sack and some chicken. Then we just find our way down to the sewers, and the monster is ours.'

Felix was still staring into the toilet. 'And why do we have to go into the sewers? Can't we, like, tempt it from up here?'

Jasper shook his head. 'I thought about that, but it would be too easy for the monster to slink back down the toilet before we grabbed it.'

'OK, but how do we actually get down to the sewers? asked Saffy.

'There must be a stormwater drain somewhere,' said Jasper. 'They use stormwater to flush out the sewerage system, so the two must be connected somehow.'

'You make it sound easy, but I have a bad feeling about this,' said Felix. 'And you're sure this is the right monster? I mean, going into the sewers is seriously gross.'

'How many eight-legged monsters do you reckon the teachers let loose every day?' Jasper replied. 'And just think, while the rest of the class spend the day digging up the icy ground, *we* know that underground means the sewers. And the bit in the clue about the button makes perfect sense. *Just a single button pressed will send me to a lengthy rest* – press the flush button, and away he goes,' said Jasper. 'But if someone has a better plan ...'

'OK,' Saffy agreed, shrugging her shoulders.

Felix sighed and nodded.

Jasper scooped a jar full of toilet water into his drink bottle, reminding himself not to use that bottle again.

'Why did you just do that?' Saffy asked, scrunching her nose at Jasper's dripping hand.

'It's all part of the plan,' he grinned, rinsing

his hands. 'And now for the Spiderman web-shooter waiting for us in the storeroom,' he added, flicking water at Saffy and Felix.

'Yeah, right,' said Felix, shutting the door firmly behind them. Saffy gave him a look.

'Just in case it, you know, comes up again,' he said.

There was a queue of kids waiting to file into the storeroom.

Felix was ahead of Jasper in the queue. 'Uh, Jasp,' he said, peering into the room. 'It's not exactly what you were hoping for.'

'This is it?' Saffy muttered as she entered the room. She picked up a box of rubber bands. 'What are we meant to do with these?'

Other kids were grabbing whatever they

could carry, and shoving it all into their packs.

'Do you think any of this will come in handy?' Felix whispered, shuffling through a box of rulers.

Jasper shook his head, 'I didn't see Mr Golag carrying any rulers with him.'

The other teams in the room were whispering to each other too: '… like the prefects used. If we aim right, we could hit its weak point without getting right up under its stomach,' Jasper overheard someone say.

'Did you hear that?' Saffy asked Jasper behind her hand. 'What do you think they mean?'

'Don't worry about it. They've got it wrong,' Jasper whispered. 'The button is the flush button. I've *seen* the monster, Saffy. Come on!'

Saffy spied a net shoved into a corner, and

Felix gave Jasper the thumbs-up as he spotted a sack on the floor.

Jasper grabbed a box of matches, some towels, three torches and a handful of paperclips, not really sure if any of it would be useful.

'Come on, let's get going,' he said to Felix, who was pulling something off the wall. 'We still need to find some chicken.'

They made their way quietly down to the kitchen. The door was locked. Jasper took two of the paperclips from his bag. He stretched them out and wriggled them into the locks. There was a soft click, and the door swung open.

'Looks like you might've done that before,' Felix said.

'Maybe a few times. How do you think I ended up at this school?'

It only took them a few minutes to raid the kitchen, adding a stash of chocolate bars

For
containing
monsters

For catching
monsters

For lighting
dark rooms

To lure the
monster

For picking
locks

For seeing

May come in
handy

marked *teachers' supplies* to the mountains of chicken they had found. They huddled around the wood-fire oven, getting warm and shoving chocolate into their mouths.

'Why do they have a pizza oven, when all we get to eat is tasteless mush and stale bread?' said Saffy, looking around.

It was a good point. Who was eating pizza around here?

No wonder the teachers and prefects don't eat in the food hall with us, Jasper thought.

He started rummaging through the pantry. There was everything needed to make good, tasty, real food. Sugar, flour, cocoa, rice, pasta, fruit, vegetables, and spices that Jasper had never heard of.

Then a large brown sack in the corner of the room caught Jasper's eye. The sack had a label that read *TO BE INCINERATED*. He wandered over and opened it.

And when he saw what was inside, he reckoned he could actually feel his blood beginning to boil.

11

'What is it?' Felix asked, peering over Jasper's shoulder.

Jasper was fuming. He felt so mad he could hardly speak. 'Letters,' he finally spat out. 'Our. Letters. Home.' He could feel his breath tightening as his anger bubbled up.

'It's a good thing I never bothered to write any, then,' Saffy said. 'Not that my parents would notice. They've probably forgotten that I exist by now and are off on another trip overseas.'

Saffy's parents were high-powered executives who had dumped her in boarding schools her whole life. But when Jasper thought about his own mum, and of all the letters he'd written her over the months, he felt betrayed.

The truth was, he had gotten used to life at Monstrum House. For once in his life he was actually enjoying school. He had great friends. It was *exciting* to catch monsters. Somehow he had started to like it here.

But this changed everything. It was a slap in the face. He knew the teachers at Monstrum House weren't exactly nice. But this was just cruel.

'Are you OK?' Felix asked quietly.

'No, not really,' Jasper replied.

Felix and Saffy looked anxiously at one another. Felix's family wasn't much of a touchy-feely letter-writing type. In fact, Felix was nearly as scared of his brothers as he was of monsters.

'They've been lying to us,' said Jasper flatly. He realised that for six months, his mum had had no idea how he was – or even *where* he was. She had told him to write whenever he could!

Jasper hadn't written the truth about Monstrum House in his letters because he didn't want to worry his mum. But now she would be worried anyway. He looked away. He didn't know if the others would understand.

'This stupid school has taken every single letter we've ever written, and burnt it,' Jasper fumed. 'They don't care about us. No matter how many monsters we catch.'

Jasper grabbed a can of dog food from the bottom of the pantry and threw it into the very back of the pizza oven. 'Let's see how their pizza tastes when that explodes,' he said.

But even the idea of the teachers eating dog-food pizza didn't make him feel any better.

Saffy laughed. 'Of course they don't care about us. The teachers hate us, didn't you notice?'

'Jasp, they make us hunt monsters,' said Felix. 'Monsters that could kill us.'

'All we've got,' said Saffy, 'is each other.'

Jasper didn't know what to do. He didn't feel like doing the Task anymore.

'Come on, Jasper. We have to use our heads,' said Saffy. 'Once we get through this Task, we'll go on a Hunt! The outside world! We'll be out of here for good. And then you can *go* home, not just write.'

'Fine,' said Jasper. 'We'll do the stupid Task and catch the Grubbergrind. And then I'm going to poke it with sticks until it's really angry. And *then*, I'll put it in the teachers' bathroom.'

Saffy grinned appreciatively.

'As long as it doesn't kill us first,' said Felix.

'Well,' Saffy said, clapping her hands. 'Now that's sorted, let's go catch a monster.'

'Where are we going?' Felix complained, as Jasper led them around the back of the mansion and along the border of the forest.

'Trust me,' Jasper said.

Felix muttered something under his breath. Jasper ignored it and led the way around the back of the school at a run. They had wasted precious time in the kitchen and their whole plan would fall apart if they didn't get to the monster first.

Given it was a trained monster, Jasper knew that the teachers wouldn't have too much trouble catching it. But he loved the idea of Stenka being surprised by a nipper-ended tentacle when she was washing her face. Their team could score some seriously good points by being the first to catch the monster, but by letting it go, Jasper would show the school that he was done with the whole stupid place.

'Jasp,' Saffy asked as they jogged, 'are you sure you know where you are going? It kind of looks like we're heading towards the kennels.'

Jasper smiled and stopped at the ring of trees that wound around the dog kennels.

Felix leant against a tree and stared at Jasper. 'The kennels?' he asked. 'Is that where the stormwater drains are?'

Jasper shook his head. 'Not quite.'

Saffy caught on first. 'A dog? You're getting a dog? I think you've finally flipped.'

Jasper motioned for her to keep quiet. They

could hear Mondrag swearing loudly as he banged a hammer. It sounded like he was fixing something around the back of the kennels.

'It's not just any dog, all right?' Jasper whispered.

The dogs were all locked in their kennels. Sniffer dogs to the left, guard dogs to the right. The sniffer dogs were mostly spaniels and wagged their tails happily as the three walked past. The guard dogs weren't quite so happy-looking. A few of them began growling.

'Sssshhhh,' Felix hissed, making more noise than the dogs. They all froze. The hammering had stopped, and Mondrag had stopped swearing.

Jasper listened intently. A dog barked.

'Quiet!' Mondrag's voice boomed from around the back and the dogs all fell silent.

Felix let his breath out slowly.

One of the guard dogs came towards Jasper, wagging his tail in greeting. 'Hey, Woof,' Jasper whispered. He grabbed a paperclip from his bag and fiddled his way into the lock on the cage.

'Keep watch,' Jasper whispered to the others. He knew Mondrag couldn't be far away. 'Come on fella, we're breaking you loose.'

Woof!

'Psst – Mondrag's coming!' Saffy said just as the lock clicked open.

There wasn't time to make it back to the cover of the trees. They flung themselves into the cage with Woof, trying to flatten themselves against the wire. Jasper glanced up and saw Mondrag turn the corner. They were stuffed. Just a few more metres and he would be on top of them.

The door to the kennel was still ajar. There was no way that Mondrag would walk past an open kennel, especially an open kennel with a dog and three students inside.

'Aaaargh,' Mondrag steamed. He was only two kennels away. He must have seen them. 'Stupid hammer!' Then he spun on his heels and headed back the way he'd come. 'I must have left it back at the fence.' Mondrag's mutterings disappeared around the corner.

Wordlessly, the kids leapt to their feet and raced out of the kennel. Woof followed them to the safety of the trees. No-one could believe their luck.

'We were so close to getting …' Jasper looked up. A dark shadow was blocking their path. 'Caught,' he finished.

'Good morning, gentlemen, young lady.' Principal Von Strasser loomed above the students. He was sitting on his huge grey horse, with a purple cape tied around his head in a sort of makeshift headdress. If he'd been carrying presents, he would have looked like one of the three wise men from a Christmas nativity scene. The horse snorted steam into the icy air, and pawed at the ground.

'Busy morning?' Von Strasser enquired.

'Ah, yes. Quite.' Saffy replied. 'We're on our first Task. You know how it is,' she added, as though she was talking to an old friend rather than the principal of Monstrum House.

Von Strasser was rarely seen. Sometimes he took a class – but Jasper, Felix and Saffy hadn't spoken with him since their first days at Monstrum House. Occasionally they would see him watching from a window – the silhouette of his plumed hat and cape impossible to mistake – but other than that, it was as if he wasn't really there.

'I was thinking of having a spot of lunch myself,' Von Strasser said. 'Perhaps some pizza – followed up by a chocolate bar or two.' He looked at Felix. 'You seem to have a bit of something on your lip there, Mr Brown.'

Felix turned a deep red and wiped the

chocolate from his face.

'The oven makes a lovely pizza – usually.'
Von Strasser looked directly at Jasper. 'but today
it smelt a little unusual.'

Jasper could feel his cheeks flush. And then
he remembered the letters. He refused to feel
guilty – not after what the school had done. 'I'm
sure it will taste great,' Jasper replied steadily.

Von Strasser nodded slightly. 'Well, my door
is always open. Feel free to drop in for tea and
a chat, any of you. I always think it's best to
get things off your chest – saves stewing apples.
Unless of course you are cooking an apple pie.
Then you *need* stewed apples.' Von Strasser
looked thoughtful. He was seriously weird.

Saffy nodded. 'We'll keep that in mind.'

Von Strasser suddenly looked surprised to
find himself in the forest talking to students.
'OK, well, cheerio,' he chirped, reaching down

to give Woof a pat on the head, before prancing away on his horse.

'Do you reckon he really is nuts?' Jasper asked once the horse had disappeared from sight.

Felix shrugged. 'I don't know. He certainly seems to know what we've been up to – but then, what was all that about stewed apples?'

Saffy was too busy laughing to answer.

'At least he didn't say anything about us dog-napping Woof,' Felix said, patting the dog.

'Right,' Saffy said, composing herself. 'Task time,' she ordered. 'Jasp – here's where you reveal your amazing plan for getting us down to the sewers.'

'Right,' said Jasper. 'Well, the thing is – I reckon that Woof and I, er, understand each other ...' he trailed off, looking sheepish.

Jasper couldn't help but notice that Felix

and Saffy looked rather sceptical.

'That's your plan?' said Saffy. 'Talk to a dog?'

'Woof,' Jasper said, ignoring Saffy and looking the dog in the eye, 'We need to get underground – into the sewers. We're looking for the toilet monster.' Jasper gingerly opened the bottle of toilet water he had saved, and let Woof have a sniff.

Saffy groaned. 'Is *that* why you've been carrying toilet water around? I can't believe –'

But Saffy didn't get to finish her sentence. Woof growled and sniffed the ground. He paused, one paw held in the air as he sniffed the wind, then raced into the forest.

Jasper smiled and charged after him. He could hear Saffy and Felix close behind him. *Good boy, Woof,* Jasper thought proudly.

Chasing a dog at top-speed through the undergrowth of an icy, snow-covered forest was hard going. Jasper could feel his feet slipping and Felix was wheezing loudly. Jasper hoped he had his asthma puffer with him.

After ten minutes of solid running, Woof stopped. Jasper, Felix and Saffy were all bent over with their hands on their knees, desperately trying to catch their breath.

'This place is seriously spooky,' Felix wheezed, as he pulled out his asthma puffer and sucked deeply. 'Monsters that eat you, teachers who know what you're thinking, prefects who terrorise you, and a dog that understands English.'

Jasper looked around him. They were standing in front of a fence with a sign that said: *EXTREME DANGER – RAPID FLOODING – DO NOT ENTER.* It was a part of the forest that none of them had seen before.

'We can't go down there,' said Felix pointing to the sign. 'Look.'

'Rapid flooding?' scoffed Saffy. 'There's not a cloud in sight.'

She was right. For once, the sun was out. The air was cold and crisp, and the snow lay on the

ground, glinting white in the sunlight.

'Let's do it.' Jasper pulled a set of bolt cutters out from his pack.

'Where did you find those?' Felix asked in amazement.

'I thought they might come in handy,' Jasper replied, cutting through the wire. 'You wait here fella,' Jasper said to Woof with a pat.

On the other side of the fence was a deep, dark ditch. It had a pipe leading underground. 'That must be the stormwater pipe,' Jasper said. 'Now our only trouble is going to be finding the pipe that leads to the sewers.'

'I might be able to help with that,' Felix said, taking his turn at looking smug. He pulled a blueprint for the underground pipe network out of his pocket. 'It was stuck on the wall of the storeroom. 'Well,' he shrugged, 'Stenka did say we could take *anything*.' He grinned and

Jasper clapped him on the back.

'Cool,' said Saffy approvingly.

'So why are we standing out here looking at the pipe?' Jasper said, pulling apart the wire on the fence, and clambering through. Saffy followed him, but Felix kept staring at the sign.

'Because it says *extreme* danger,' he called.

Saffy and Jasper just smiled. 'Come on, you know you'll miss us. And you'll be all alone out here … ' Saffy called back.

Felix took a deep breath and followed the others towards the pipe.

When Jasper thought of what was lurking somewhere in these pipes, he felt a familiar buzz mixed with an inkling of fear.

It was dark and wet in the stormwater drain.

And it really stank. Jasper's feet were soaked with stuff he didn't want to think about. He wished they had thought of gumboots.

As Felix had the blueprints, he led the way through the maze of pipes, his torch flashing off the walls around them. Rats scuttled near their feet, screeching if anyone came too close.

'I hate rats!' Felix moaned, sloshing through the water, trying not to step on any. Jasper crept up behind him and squeaked loudly in his ear, making Felix drop his torch into the water.

'Uh-oh,' said Jasper, rescuing the torch from the stinky water. He tried it, but it was dead.

'Good one, Jasper,' said Saffy. 'Now it's even harder to see what's coming. Here, Felix, have mine.'

The further in they went, the worse the smell became.

'That pipe there –' Felix shone the torch

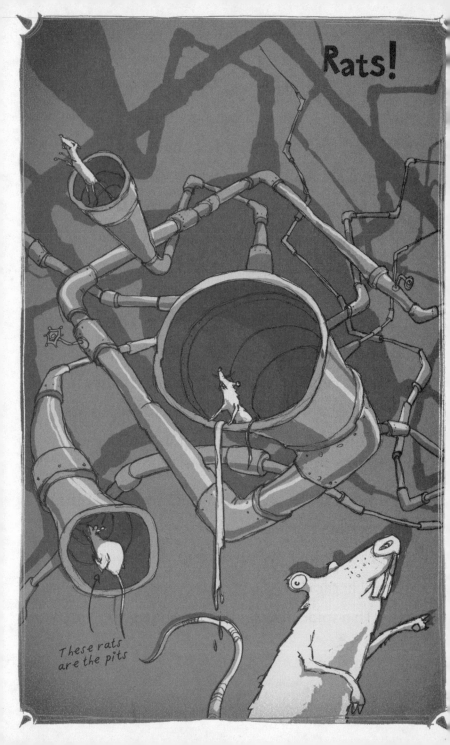

Rats!

These rats are the pits

down a pipe that lead back towards the school. He looked at the blueprints. 'I'm pretty sure that's the one that leads to the sewerage system. It smells bad enough.'

They all had their faces covered with their sleeves. It didn't do any good.

Jasper tried to build a mental image of the school grounds and the pipes they had passed so far.

Hang on … Pipes! Jasper had an idea. He couldn't believe he hadn't thought of it before.

He stopped walking. The others stopped too, Felix nervously shining his torch along the walls. 'You know all this water has to go somewhere,' said Jasper.

The others looked at him blankly.

'Well, obviously,' said Saffy.

'I mean, somewhere *outside the school*,' Jasper replied.

'Ooh!' said Saffy as she realised what Jasper was getting at.

Suddenly Jasper didn't care about letting the Grubbergrind loose. It seemed silly to even catch a stupid monster, when they could all escape Monstrum House, right now.

'What?' said Felix.

'We could always just – well – you know, *keep going*,' said Jasper. The thought of freedom raced through his head. He couldn't stop grinning.

Felix shone the torch in Jasper's face. 'Are you serious?'

Jasper shielded his eyes from the torch beam. 'We have twenty-four hours. They won't notice we're missing for the whole time we are meant to be on the Task, and by then we'll be long gone.'

Saffy was nodding. 'It's brilliant!'

'No more monsters!' Felix realised.

'No more teachers!' Saffy added.

'No more punishments!' Saffy and Felix said at the same time.

'Although … ' Felix trailed off. Jasper wondered if he was thinking about their rather painful escape attempt earlier in the year, when Felix and Saffy had been morphed into stone statues by a Bogglemorph.

'Come on, Felix,' Saffy said, 'it's not like you're safe from monsters if you stay at school. And besides, if we run into anything, Jasper can take it on this time. And then, once we're out of here, hunting monsters won't be your problem anymore!'

'Let's do it,' Jasper said.

Felix sighed and shrugged. 'OK,' he said.

Jasper thought it wouldn't take long to get past the school boundary going along the pipes. Then they could climb up a manhole, and into freedom. Relief flooded his body.

Jasper wasn't exactly sure what was outside the Monstrum House school grounds. They could be anywhere, really. But he didn't care. He didn't care about any of it anymore.

They kept walking along the drain. Shadows flashed in and out of the torch beams. Their footsteps echoed along the pipes as they splashed through the drain.

'Freedom – here we come!' Saffy called, her voice bouncing off the walls.

Suddenly, Jasper heard it again. That same hissing whisper. *Kuuumm … Jassssppeeer …* it whispered. *Naaah … kuuum ….* Jasper felt his guts clench into a tight ball.

'Did either of you hear that?' he asked.

'Hear what?' said Felix.

'All I can hear is victory calling,' Saffy replied happily, splashing her way past Jasper.

Jasper tried to shake the feeling of dread away, but it stuck. Something was talking to him, and he didn't know what.

Jasper, Felix and Saffy continued along the tunnel. It seemed to be growing darker. Maybe their torches were running out of batteries?

'Shhh,' said Felix. 'I can hear something.'

'The whispering, yeah?' asked Jasper.

'No, it's more like a squelching.'

They all stopped to listen, but the sound was gone. Felix shrugged and checked the blueprint again. 'This way,' he said, bravely taking the lead. He turned around the corner into another pipe. Saffy and Jasper followed close behind.

As they rounded the corner, Saffy and Jasper smacked straight into Felix, who had stopped dead in his tracks.

'Um, change of plans,' whispered Felix.

There, squelched in front of them, was the Grubbergrind. It thrashed its tentacles in the air as it moved towards them. It looked bigger than when Jasper had seen it dropped into the toilet. In fact, Jasper wasn't sure how it had even fitted down there.

'Perhaps the rats aren't so bad after all,' Felix whispered.

Saffy slowly pulled the net from her back-pack. 'Easy now,' she cooed. Jasper and Felix stayed frozen to the spot. The Grubbergrind looked like some sort of mutant octopus. A mutant octopus that ate people. Maybe that's why it had grown. Had it eaten another Task team?

The Grubbergrind

Sharp nippers!

Mind the weird shrinking goo!

Species: Grubbergrind
Order: Muncher

Saffy crept in closer to the monster, keeping just out of reach of its giant nipper-ended tentacles. She raised the net over its head. The Grubbergrind seemed to smile. Jasper didn't know monsters could smile.

As Saffy's net came down over the monster's head, it opened its mouth wide and shot a long line of goo towards her. The goo went straight through the netting and hit Saffy squarely in the face.

There was a tense moment as everyone waited to see what would happen. 'Gross,' said Saffy, wiping the goo out of her eyes.

'Does it taste like fish?' Jasper asked.

But Saffy didn't reply. Instead, she began to shrink. Bit by bit.

Her arms shrank first, and Saffy yelled in surprise as her arms shrank to the size of two pins. Then the determined look on her face grew smaller as her head shrank away. There was a POP, and her body shrank to the size of an orange pip. Saffy was nothing more than a pair of legs with a miniature body and head attached. And then, with a *swoosh*, her legs seemed to wind in on themselves, and Saffy was no more than the size of a fly.

And drowning in the stinky water.

'Saffy!' screamed Felix and Jasper together.

Jasper didn't stop to think. He stretched his arm towards the flailing Saffy. He picked her up on his finger, like you would a caterpillar. He was relieved to see she looked OK. Trying to resuscitate someone that small would have been tricky.

'Aaaaargh!' Felix yelled in some kind of war cry. Jasper looked up just in time to see Felix fly at the monster and deliver a fierce karate kick at its head.

'Go Felix!' he yelled, forgetting about Saffy for a moment and almost dropping her. A tiny sharp bite to his finger brought him back to his senses.

Jasper had felt the force of Felix's karate kicks before, and didn't think the blubbery octopus had a chance.

That was, until Felix's leg bounced off the monster and he was instantly covered in swirling goo. Felix gave Jasper a look of despair, before following Saffy's performance of shrinking bit by bit into the water.

Jasper knew that if he got shot by goo, they would all drown. He grabbed Felix's tiny body from the water and put both Felix and Saffy into his hoodie pocket. Then he reached carefully into his pack.

'Chicken, my beauty?' he growled, doing his best impersonation of Mr Golag. Jasper remembered the tender look that had crossed Mr Golag's face when he looked at the monster, and tried to imagine himself feeling the same sort of affection for something so horrible. The Grubbergrind closed its mouth and cocked its head to one side.

Jasper pulled out an entire roast chicken from his bag and threw it towards the monster. The Grubbergrind grabbed the chicken in its tentacles and quickly sucked the bones dry.

Jasper hurriedly threw more and more chicken to the monster. But it wasn't slowing down, and Jasper was going to run out of chicken at this rate. He grabbed the sack and opened it wide.

'There's more chicken inside, my beauty,' he growled. The Grubbergrind looked at Jasper again. It opened its mouth. Jasper wondered what would happen to his friends if he was shrunk. Would they shrink again? Would they even exist? How small could something get before it just 'poofed' away?

Jasper waited for the goo to come – but it didn't. The Grubbergrind squelched its way towards the sack, jumping along on its nippered tentacles. It tried to push inside the sack, but it was far too big.

The monster started oozing goo out of the suckers on its tentacles. Jasper held his breath. Then the monster began to rub the goo over its own body, and it started shrinking until it was the size of a large cat. It leapt inside the sack, looking for more chicken.

It must really like chicken, thought Jasper, tying the string securely. He hoped that the goo couldn't get through the sack. All he could hear was more chewing. The monster seemed happy – for now.

But what about Felix and Saffy? thought Jasper. *Will the teachers be able to unshrink them? What sort of life will they have as mini people? Are there any mini monster-hunting schools?*

Jasper thought of their escape plan. The pipes looked so – well, inviting wasn't the word – but still, freedom lay at the end of one of them

He grabbed his friends out of his pocket. 'Which pipe is the way out, Felix?' All he heard was an angry high-pitched squeak as Felix waved what looked like a very tiny set of blueprints at him.

'What is it with you two getting Monstered every time we try to escape?' sighed Jasper.

It was no use. There was only one chance of getting his friends back to their normal size. And it was at Monstrum House. The teachers would know what to do.

Jasper put his friends carefully back into his

pocket, and heaved the wriggling monster-sack onto his back.

He hurried back along the maze of pipes the way they'd come. He took a few wrong turns, and at one point wondered if he would ever find his way out.

But after what felt like hours of racing through stinking water by torchlight, Jasper finally saw the light at the end of the tunnel. He checked his watch. It was late in the afternoon. Soon it would be getting dark.

He had to get back to school, and get his friends back to size.

15

Jasper crept out of the stormwater pipe and into the ditch. While they were in the drain, clouds had come over and now thunder rumbled through the sky. The afternoon had darkened and sleety, icy rain came tumbling down.

He hated to think what might have happened if they'd still been in the stormwater drain.

He ran along the ditch towards the fence. The heavy monster-sack bumped against his back.

'Perhaps it's a good thing we didn't try to escape,' Jasper said to his tiny friends. He heard

Saffy squeaking something back at him. 'If you were still normal-sized, we would probably be in the sewers right now. That monster might have just saved our lives.'

More squeaks made Jasper think his mini friends weren't feeling very grateful.

The Grubbergrind wobbled about in the sack on Jasper's back, but didn't seem to be too distressed. *Perhaps he thinks I really am Mr Golag,* thought Jasper.

The rain was pelting down now, turning the ditch into a mudslide. Jasper tried to clamber his way out through the fence, but with the sack in his hands it was useless.

The third time Jasper fell down in the mud, he heard his friends squeak angrily from his pocket. 'Sorry!' Jasper shouted, probably a bit too loudly for their tiny ears.

He needed to find another place where he

could climb over the fence and back into the forest.

He followed the fence line until he came to a place where the wire was completely mangled. It looked as though it had been bashed by something huge. Or gnashed. Or sliced. Or …

Jasper stopped thinking about it. Climbing through here would be easier than fiddling around with the bolt cutters in the dark and wet somewhere else along the fence.

The ground was overrun with tree roots. Jasper used one as a foothold and scrambled up, pulling himself under the fence and into the forest undergrowth.

'At least I don't have to worry about monsters,' Jasper said to the sack. 'I already have you.'

Jasper heaved the wriggling sack back onto his back, feeling pleased with himself at having successfully completed the Task. Successful, that is, if you didn't count the size of his tiny team-mates.

He made his way into the darkening forest towards the school.

And then he saw it.

Standing in front of Jasper, was the biggest, most horrible spider he had ever seen. And it had eight long spindly legs.

Technically, this wasn't just the most horrible spider Jasper had ever seen – it was worse than that. It was a spider-monster. Jasper started to shake.

OK, deep breath, Jasper commanded himself.

'Um, guys, we have a slight problem,' Jasper said to the tiny friends in his pocket. 'There's a spider. Well, it isn't really a spider, it's …' but Jasper didn't know what it was.

It had a hairy body and a whole bunch of eyes like other spiders – but it also had wings on its back, rows and rows of sharp fangs, and legs that ended in talons, like you'd see on a vulture. And it was the size of an army tank.

'It's my worst nightmare,' Jasper whispered.

He could make out the entrance to a large lair behind the monster. The lair was covered in a white, sticky spider web, and behind it were the terrified faces of Class 1B.

'JASPER! GET US OUT OF HERE!' they yelled as soon as they saw him.

The spider-monster raised its fangs, revealing a blistered yellow tongue oozing with blue pus.

'WHAT IS IT? AND WHAT IS IT DOING HERE?' Jasper yelled.

'IT'S THE GRUBBERGRIND!' a voice yelled.

'CATCH IT!' yelled someone else.

Home-made slingshots littered the ground around the lair. Suddenly the rubber bands and rulers in the storeroom made sense.

'Hang on,' Jasper said. 'But I *have* the Grubbergrind.'

He looked down at the sack in his hands. Then back up at the spider-monster. Its gleaming eyes were fixed on him. Jasper could see his face reflected in every eye – and he couldn't help but notice the look of utter confusion in every reflection. It took Jasper a few moments to work things out.

'But if … if *that* is the Grubbergrind …' Jasper trailed off, *then I haven't caught the Grubbergrind after all,* he realised. *I just have some random toilet monster in my sack, two mini friends in my pocket, a whole bunch of classmates trapped in a lair, and a monster waiting to catch me.*

And it's a Muncher, he reminded himself, looking at its gleaming fangs.

Suddenly, Jasper felt very cold. The Grubbergrind had moved without a sound. It was right above of him. It lifted its front legs, twirling a ball of web down towards him.

Jasper took a deep breath. Despair filled his body. He didn't even scream. He was done for.

Jasper watched in horror as the Grubbergrind – the real one this time – reared its front legs above its head. In some part of his brain, a soothing voice told him that he wouldn't actually be killed, just trapped like the rest of the class.

But the rest of his brain broke out into a cold panic. DONE FOR. DONE FOR. BIG SPIDER. GONER.

And my life isn't even flashing before my eyes, Jasper thought. He felt kind of ripped off. If he was going to die, he might as well do it properly.

Species: Grubbergrind,
Order: Muncher

The REAL Grubbergrind

A sharp bark broke through Jasper's thoughts. The Grubbergrind froze, a few centimetres from Jasper's shaking body. There was another bark, followed by a deep, guttural growl. Jasper didn't move a muscle.

The Grubbergrind stepped backwards, whirring its wings angrily as it backed away from the approaching dog.

Woof had his teeth bared at the monster. He really looked like a ferocious guard dog. Woof pounced, and sank his teeth into the monster's abdomen. But even a dog as big as Woof was no match for a tank-sized, fanged, winged, taloned spider-monster.

It is still a monster with monstrous instincts, Stenka had said. Jasper figured it would be pretty happy to eat a dog.

Woof didn't stand a chance.

Feeling panicked, Jasper thought about

everything he had in his pack. *Paperclips? Useless. Bolt cutters? No good. Chicken? Chocolate bars? No … I think Munchers prefer live bait.*

So much for being prepared.

And then something in Jasper's brain clicked. He did have a weapon! He opened the sack.

'Do this,' Jasper whispered to the toilet monster, 'and there's a whole load more chicken for you.' He really hoped the monster understood.

Jasper reached inside and pulled the monster out by its slimy, wart-covered head. The monster didn't look too pleased, but it didn't shoot goo at him.

'Get back, Woof!' Jasper yelled. 'NOW!' he shouted, giving the toilet monster a squeeze. The monster obeyed, opening its mouth wide and spraying goo all over the Grubbergrind.

The Grubbergrind froze. There was complete

silence. And then, before everyone's eyes, it began to shrink, leg by leg, eye by eye, talon by horrible talon, right down to the size of a small spider. Well, a small spider with wings, fangs and talons.

Before it had a chance to escape, Jasper grabbed a box of matches from their supplies, emptied it out and clapped it over the shrunken monster. Then, he carefully slid the matchbox lid back over the box.

The Grubbergrind was trapped.

'Not a spider, not a spider, not a spider,' Jasper whispered to himself, and shoved it deep into the pocket of his hoodie.

Then he remembered Saffy and Felix! He ripped the matchbox out again, and put it in his other pocket, then zipped it firmly shut. His friends would definitely be angry now.

Jasper smiled at the toilet monster and patted

its slimy head. 'Thanks, fella. You're not so bad after all.'

Jasper thought the toilet monster looked almost cute. It blobbed at him cheerfully and wound a tentacle lovingly around his hand.

'Hmm, OK, let's just put you back …' Jasper untangled his arm and gently placed the toilet monster back into the sack.

Woof limped over to Jasper, licking his hand. The Grubbergrind had cut a gash in his leg with a talon but, other than that, he seemed fine.

Jasper knelt down and hugged the dog. 'You're a good boy,' he said.

Jasper was pulled back to reality by a voice shouting at him from inside the monster's lair.

'Come on, Jasper!' called one of his classmates. 'We're still stuck here, you know!'

A sudden crack of thunder made the trapped kids yell even more frantically.

Jasper pulled the bolt cutters from his pack, and cut through the thick strands of sticky white webbing. When he was done, the captured kids burst out of the lair, hugged him, and sprinted back towards the mansion as if it was not such a bad place to be after all.

Jasper made a mental note to ask them later how they had worked out the clue. He had the feeling that this was one mistake Saffy and Felix wouldn't let him forget in a hurry.

Jasper stood to attention in front of Stenka's desk. It was hard to tell exactly how angry she was because she wasn't yelling – she was staring icily at him. She picked up the stick she usually used for pointing, and snapped it in half.

'Mr McPhee,' she said coolly. 'You're lucky we have an antidote for Octoglug goo. It's not something we always keep on hand. You might have thought of that *before* shrinking your friends to the size of beetles.'

Jasper was about to argue that *he* hadn't

actually shrunk them, but then he saw the way Stenka's eyes flashed with anger.

Jasper had watched as Stenka had administered the antidote. If his friends thought being shrunk was bad, it was nothing compared to being un-shrunk. They had grown, as they had shrunk, one bit at a time. Their tiny little bodies grew green gooey legs, then their torsos glooped out of their legs, their heads and arms slopped into place, and finally there was a POP! The gooey jelly set hard, and they were both back to normal.

Except that they were covered in goo, and coughing up great gobs of it from their lungs. Jasper couldn't tell if it was worse than when they had been de-morphed from being stone statues. It looked less painful, but more disgusting. Still, at least they were OK now, apart from the occasional gooey sneeze. Felix's voice had a distinct high-pitched squeak to it, but apparently that wouldn't last for too long.

Jasper was pulled back to the present by Stenka's frosty voice. 'We take theft seriously at Monstrum House. Dog-napping from Mondrag's kennels. Stealing an Octoglug from the sewer.' Her eyes hardened. 'How could you possibly think that the clues could refer to an *Octoglug*? Did you consider why the clues were delivered by slingshot? Did you even *read* the clues? Have you completely forgotten about those monsters whose weakness is their bellybutton? A simple blow to the Grubbergrind's bellybutton would have sent it into a deep sleep!'

Jasper vaguely remembered something Stenka had said in one of their first classes about weaknesses ... but as for the slingshots, he'd just thought that was the prefects' way of having fun. Although it looked like Felix had been right about the poem. If only they had found the right eight-legged monster.

'Octoglugs don't creep and crawl, they squelch and jump! Or didn't you notice that?' Stenka hissed.

Jasper squirmed. 'Well, now that you mention it …' he mumbled.

'Octoglugs don't even eat people!' Stenka continued. 'Mr Golag is not happy. That monster was meant to clear the pipes. Since you stole it, the pipes have already blocked up. He's put your name down on the list of students to clean the bathrooms.'

So *that* was what the monster had been doing. Only at Monstrum House would teachers put monsters in the toilets to keep them clean.

'And then there is the breaking and entering and vandalism,' continued Stenka.

Jasper remembered the letters to be

146

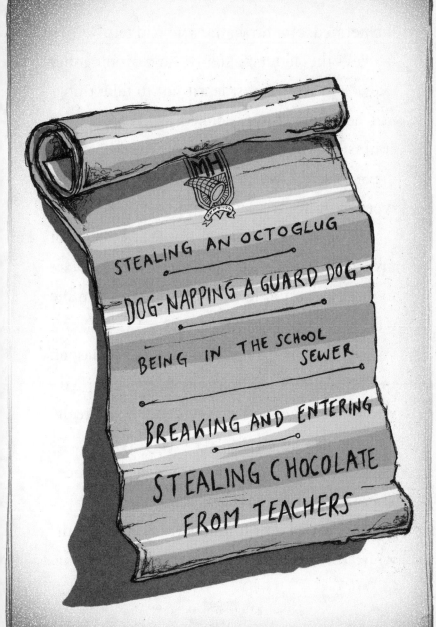

incinerated, and how angry he had felt.

'Yes, the letters,' Stenka said, rolling her eyes. 'You really must learn not to take things at face value.' Jasper looked at his teacher in confusion. 'What do you think would happen if parents received letters home detailing the types of things we do here, hmm?'

Jasper shook his head. 'But that's not what my letters said!' he said angrily. 'My letters were to make my mum feel better. To make sure she wouldn't worry! And now –'

Stenka held up her hand to silence Jasper. 'And your mother received every letter you wrote. We have the video evidence if you really feel the need to watch.'

Jasper was speechless. Video evidence? There were cameras in his house?

'The letters you found were from students who didn't think about what they were writing.

The students who would have ended up in mental institutions had they reported what really goes on here.'

Jasper had assumed that *all* of their letters were destroyed.

'And, for your information, all those students affected were told that their parents wouldn't be receiving their original letters. They were encouraged to write a more, shall we say, *believable* version of events.'

Jasper let his gaze drop. Perhaps it was a good thing he hadn't been able to let the monster loose.

'Principal Von Strasser asked me to remind you of his invitation to join him for apple pie. He also wanted me to give you this.'

Stenka reached into her desk drawer and pulled out a folder marked:

Student Intake File.

149

'You were meant to review this earlier in the year. If you remember, Principal Von Strasser took you to the records room?' she said, handing him the folder.

Jasper remembered. That was just before he had tried to escape Monstrum House and ended up running head-first into a Bogglemorph. A lot had happened since then, and he had completely forgotten about the file.

Jasper flipped the file open. A photo stared up at him. The name on the file said *Scarlett Maitland*. His mother's maiden name.

'Mum?' Jasper gasped, looking up at Stenka.

Stenka nodded. 'Yes. Your mother attended Monstrum House. She was a talented student.'

'But she ... she ... never said ...' Jasper could only stare numbly at the photo.

'Did you not wonder why your mother soaks her feet in ice-cold water?'

'I always thought she just had sore feet,' he replied.

His brain was firing a million messages at him. He felt completely confused. His mother? Here? At Monstrum House?

'Of course, after the incident, we expected you would follow in your mother's footsteps. But your mother was certainly not as much trouble as you are proving to be.'

What incident? thought Jasper. But Stenka's face was stony.

'I think that's enough information for one day,' Stenka said, pulling the file from Jasper's hand and slapping it back into the desk drawer. 'And now, I think we will return to the charges of breaking and entering,' she continued. 'I said you could use anything from Storeroom A. I don't recall saying anything about breaking into the kitchen and stealing supplies.'

Jasper wondered if he could just keep quiet, but Stenka was staring at him, waiting for him to speak.

'Well, to be fair,' he began, 'you never said *not* to break in and steal supplies.'

Stenka's face turned a deep shade of red, and Jasper wondered if it were possible for eyes to actually pop out of someone's head.

Stenka didn't say anything for a moment. And then she did exactly what Jasper feared the most: she smiled. 'Well done,' she said.

Wha–? Was she being sarcastic? Was she going to keep him in the basement with the Blibberwail forever?

'I don't think you quite realise what you did today. No-one has ever made it through their first Task. In the entire history of Monstrum House,' Stenka said. 'You're not *meant* to make it through. We set you up with an impossible task so that you all start to take your monster-hunting duties seriously. The Task is intended to rank students from the most able to the least able, but we don't expect anyone to actually complete it. It's a remarkable achievement.'

Jasper was confused. Did this mean she wasn't angry?

'Just imagine if no-one hunted monsters,' Stenka said. 'Imagine the chaos! You kids – misfits in the outside world – are the only hope. We need kids with courage, who are prepared to break rules to get things done. Like you did today. Kids who will go the whole way.'

Jasper couldn't believe it. She was actually congratulating him. No-one was ever going to believe this.

'Of course, there is still your punishment to discuss.'

This was more like the Stenka he knew.

He was almost relieved. Stenka being nice was seriously unnerving.

'While you did complete the Task, you broke a number of rules along the way.' She paused. 'However, given that you single-handedly captured the Grubbergrind, I think a fairly light punishment is in order.'

Jasper nodded eagerly. A fairly light punishment sounded good to him.

Stenka sighed. 'According to my calculations, penalty points for all the rules you broke today add up to at least 120 points. Luckily for you, I have not had a chance to change the punishment board. This means for your 120 points, you will spend six nights running the penalty course. The rest of the class will be running the penalty course for six nights for failing the Task. You will join them. Dismissed.'

Jasper nodded and quietly made his way out

of Stenka's office. He couldn't believe he'd got off so lightly. And even though he knew six nights of running would be exhausting, Jasper had to smile.

After all, he knew the shortcut.

TO BE CONTINUED...